This edition published 2020

Folk Tale written by Molly Willett

Illustrations by Hannah Garland

Printed in the UK

GUY'S ADVENTURES

WRITTEN BY MOLLY WILLETT ILLUSTRATED BY HANNAH GARLAND

munch

"It's really boring being a shepherd" complained Guy as he looked at his fluffy sheep chewing the grass just like they always did.
Every day.
Munch, munch, munch.
"It's not like being a prince or something cool like that"
He sighed "I just wish I could have an adventure that's all"

The very next day, when Guy was still in bed, he felt the ground begin to shake. It growled and grumbled like it was hungry. Guy watched out of the windows as one by one his sheep just disappeared before his eyes.

He jumped up in shock. He had never experienced an earthquake before but he was pretty sure that they weren't supposed to make sheep vanish! So, he pulled on his trousers and ran outside.

Just as he was about to reach the spot where his sheep had disappeared, he skidded to a halt, his toes dangling over the edge of a massive hole in the ground. The hole was deep and dark but he could hear his sheep bleating from below.

Guy took a deep breath, he had wanted adventure after all. He jumped.

Darkness surrounded him as he tumbled down and down into the hole. He landed with a thump on the dusty floor.

Looking around he saw that all of his sheep were happily looking for grass among the piles of gold that were spread all around a giant golden horse. Guy stood there confused- he had never seen so much gold in his life. He walked towards the horse.

As he approached he noticed something gleaming; attached to its reins was the most beautiful ring Guy had ever seen. It had a gold band and was set with a blood red ruby that was reflecting the light.

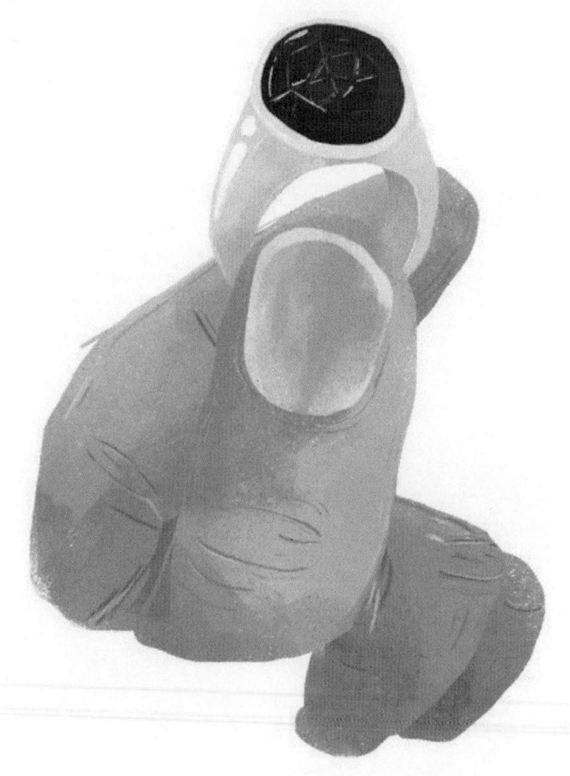

Guy could feel his heart pounding. He heard one of the other shepherds calling him from above. He quickly untied the ring and slid it onto his finger.

Having climbed back out of the hole, he looked for his friends to tell them about the gold...and to get help pulling his sheep back up to the grass before they got too hungry.

He found all the other shepherds in a clearing looking sad. He was so excited to tell them about the gold - that was sure to cheer them up.

He ran into the middle of the group and started to explain loudly and excitedly all about the adventure that he had had that morning. But none of the other shepherds seemed interested, none of them even looked at him.

"Well that's just rude" fumed Guy. He couldn't understand why none of them were interested when he was trying to make them all rich. With all that gold, they could have fun and go on adventures; even the sheep could live in posh houses if they wanted.

One of the older shepherds began speaking, "This is a sad day, the earthquake has taken all of our sheep from us and even poor Guy is lost, what shall we do?"

Guy tried to tell the others that he was there, but no one seemed to hear him. He started to shout, he danced a silly dance but still no one paid any attention.

And then he realised. He must be invisible. He couldn't think of any other explanation.

He started to panic, he didn't want to be invisible forever. Why couldn't he have been happy as a shepherd without adventure?

He took the ring off and was about to throw it in the grass when all the other shepherds gasped. They could see him again. They gathered round to ask if he was okay.

He explained where the sheep were and how they could all be rich...but he didn't mention the ring.

While the other shepherds were busy collecting the gold, and trying to pull the sheep out of the hole (which was surprisingly difficult because they kept jumping back in), Guy put the ring back on.

Time for another adventure he thought as he headed towards the palace.

The palace was big and splendid, with jewels and paintings everywhere. He wandered down large hallways and through impressive rooms without being stopped by the guards.

He was about to take an apple from the king's fruit bowl, when he heard someone sighing. It reminded him of how he had felt watching the sheep day after day; surely no one who lived in a palace could be that sad.

He rounded the corner to see the princess, she was hanging upside down and throwing a ball against the wall repeatedly. she looked really quite grumpy.

Guy was annoyed. She had everything, she shouldn't be sad! So, he took the ring off and was about to tell her to stop being miserable when her ball hit him square in the face. The princess laughed and congratulated herself on an excellent shot.

Guy rubbed his sore nose. "are you not even going to ask how I appeared from nowhere?"

"Nope" said the princess turning herself up the right way "Do you want to play a game?"

He reluctantly agreed and they started playing catch; she was very good. She jumped and dived and didn't miss a single one.

He quickly realised that the Princess was just bored and lonely, like he had been, so he promised that he would come and see her again.

He came back day after day, they become good friends and he even decided that he would show her the ring.

She thought it was amazing!

Soon they were taking turns becoming invisible and scaring the guards by making things 'float'. They even sneaked into the throne room and she let Guy try on one of her crowns.

"I wish I was a prince" said Guy as he looked at his reflection in the super fancy mirror, and swished his imaginary robe.

"What?" Gasped the princess "Why would you want to be a prince when you already have the coolest job ever??"

"I'm. A. Shepherd." He spoke the words like he was talking to someone a little bit dim.

"Oh I know" she said brightly "I'd love to be a shepherd, you must have so many friends and get to play with all the sheep. I'm jealous."

Guy stared at her open mouthed. She was jealous… of him?!?

"Yes, really I am! Oh, please take me to see your sheep, I just want to go on an adventure!"

So he did.

And as he watched her run through the grass and teach the sheep to dance, he had to admit that being a shepherd could be pretty cool after all...

Printed in Great Britain
by Amazon